Mitchellville
Elementary Library

America's Game
St. Louis Cardinals

CHRIS W. SEHNERT

ABDO & Daughters
PUBLISHING

Published by Abdo & Daughters, 4940 Viking Dr., Suite 622, Edina, MN 55435.

Copyright ©1997 by Abdo Consulting Group, Inc., Pentagon Tower, P.O. Box 36036, Minneapolis, Minnesota 55435. International copyrights reserved in all countries. No part of this book may be reproduced in any form without written permission from the publisher. Printed in the United States.

Cover photo: Allsport
Interior photos: Archive Photos: 1, 8, 14, 20
　　　　　　　　Wide World Photo: 5, 10-13, 15-17, 21-28

Edited by Paul Joseph

Library of Congress Cataloging–in–Publication Data

Sehnert, Chris W.
　St. Louis Cardinals / Chris W. Sehnert
　　　p. cm. — (America's game)
　Includes index.
　Summary: Focuses on key players and events in the history of the St. Louis Cardinals, a team which dates back to 1882.
　ISBN　1-56239-662-5
　1. St. Louis Cardinals (Baseball team)—Juvenile literature.
[1. St. Louis Cardinals (Baseball team)　2. Baseball—History.]
I. Title.　II. Series.
GV875.S3S45　1996
796.357'64'0977866—dc20　　　　　　　　　96-5576
　　　　　　　　　　　　　　　　　　　　　　　　CIP
　　　　　　　　　　　　　　　　　　　　　　　　AC

Contents

St. Louis Cardinals 4

Brown Stockings 6

Down On The Farm 7

Rajah 9

Frankie Frisch 10

The Gashouse Gang 12

Enos & The Man 17

New Owner 22

Come To See The Wizard 25

Tradition Of Excellence 28

Glossary 29

Index 31

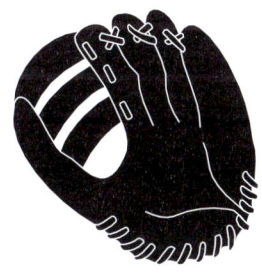

St. Louis Cardinals

The St. Louis Cardinals baseball team is one of the most successful organizations in professional sports. Their long history includes more championships than any other team in National League (NL) history.

The story of the Cardinals begins in the nineteenth century. Known as the Brown Stockings in their early days, they became the only members of the old American Association to win a World Series. After joining the NL, they became known as the St. Louis Perfectos for one year, before changing their name one last time.

Major League Baseball's record book is filled with the achievements of Cardinal players. From the great Rogers Hornsby to the incredible Ozzie Smith, the tradition of excellence in St. Louis has been maintained. Along the way, the "Gashouse Gang," Stan Musial, Lou Brock, and Bob Gibson have provided some of baseball's greatest memories.

Today, the Cardinals continue their quest for excellence with young stars like Brian Jordan, Bernard Gilkey, and Ray Lankford. Each new season brings the hope of raising another NL Pennant to fly high above St. Louis.

Ozzie Smith leaps over Todd Hundley of the New York Mets to complete a double play.

Brown Stockings

Major League Baseball is tied to its past through historic organizations. A handful of these clubs remain today, more than a century after professional baseball began. The St. Louis Cardinals' organization dates back to 1882. That year, the Brown Stockings became charter members of the new American Association (AA).

The AA was formed as a rival to the older NL, which was established in 1876. The Brown Stockings played ten seasons in the AA, and won the league's pennant four times. When the AA folded after the 1891 season, St. Louis joined the NL.

St. Louis won their first AA Pennant in 1885. The Nineteenth Century version of the World Series featured a match between the champions of the AA and the NL. Chicago's White Stockings won the 1885 NL Pennant, and met St. Louis in the post-season.

The 1885 World Series ended in a tie (3-3-1). St. Louis' three victories in the series brought respect for the young AA.

The next year, the Brown Stockings received more than respect. They became the first and only AA team to win a World Championship. They defeated the White Stockings in the 1886 World Series.

The Brown Stockings carried their pennant winning streak to four straight by winning it in 1887 and 1888.

In 1887, St. Louis lost the World Series to the NL's Detroit Wolverines. The following year, St. Louis won their final AA Pennant, but were defeated in the World Series by the New York Giants.

Down On The Farm

The Brown Stockings moved to the NL in 1892. Their roster was combined with the Cleveland Spiders in 1899, and they became known as the Perfectos. The following season they were renamed the St. Louis Cardinals.

The Cardinals were headed for bankruptcy when they hired Branch Rickey to run the ball club in 1916. St. Louis could not afford to purchase the top talent. So Rickey decided that hiring scouts and developing talent would work better for the Cardinals. He invented the farm system.

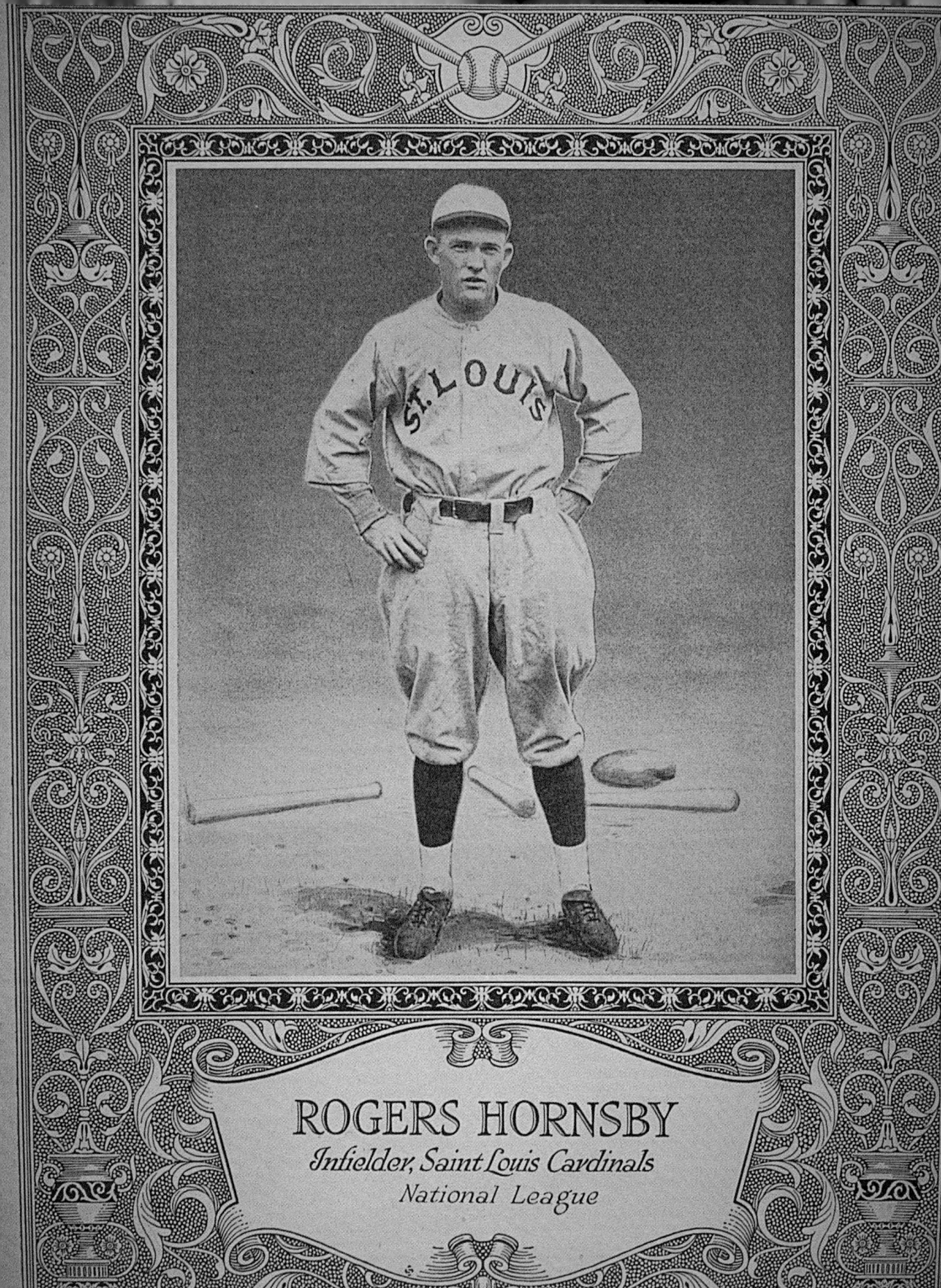

ROGERS HORNSBY
Infielder, Saint Louis Cardinals
National League

Rajah

Branch Rickey's farm system pulled the Cardinals' organization out of debt. It also produced Hall-of-Fame ballplayers for the team.

In 1920, the Cardinals moved into Sportsman's Park. They shared the stadium with their crosstown rivals, the American League's (AL's) St. Louis Browns.

The Cardinals promoted first baseman Jim Bottomley from their farm system in 1922. Two years later, they brought up outfielder Charles "Chick" Hafey. In 1925, St. Louis gave the job of manager to their veteran second baseman, Rogers Hornsby.

"Rajah," as Hornsby was known, joined the Cardinals in 1915, before the farm system was in place. A scouting report said Hornsby "couldn't hit a lick" in the minors, but he was signed for his defensive ability. He became the greatest right-handed hitter in baseball history.

Beginning in 1920, Hornsby won the NL batting crown six years in a row. His combined batting average was .397 during that period! His .424 batting average in 1924 remains the highest in modern baseball history.

As manager, Hornsby led the Cardinals to their first NL Pennant in 1926. Jim Bottomley led the league in RBIs with 120, and had 40 doubles that season. St. Louis finished two games in front of the Cincinnati Reds.

The Cardinals faced the powerful New York Yankees in the 1926 World Series. Hall-of-Fame pitcher Grover Cleveland "Pete" Alexander was traded to the Cardinals in mid-season. He was a key element in the team's World Championship.

Facing page: Rogers Hornsby on an old-time baseball card.

Frankie Frisch, shown here in 1934.

Frankie Frisch

Frankie Frisch came to the Cardinals from the New York Giants, where he was the second baseman on four straight NL Pennant winners. He was under intense pressure, during the 1927 season in St. Louis, to fill the shoes of Hornsby, who was traded. While the Cardinals did not repeat as NL champions, Frankie batted .337 and led the league in stolen bases with 48.

The Cardinals won the 1928 NL Pennant by two games over the New York Giants. Jim Bottomley led the league with 20 triples, 31 home runs (HRs), and 136 RBIs, and was elected the NL's Most Valuable Player (MVP). Chick Hafey finished right behind Bottomley on offense, and provided a powerful arm in center field. Frisch led the league in fielding average for the second straight year.

The Cardinals faced the New York Yankees, who won their third straight AL Pennant in 1928. The Yankees overpowered the Cardinals in the World Series.

After a disappointing season in 1929, the Redbirds returned to win back-to-back NL Pennants in 1930 and 1931. Pitcher "Wild Bill" Hallahan led the league in strikeouts both years. In 1931, Hallahan also led the NL with 19 wins. Chick Hafey took the 1931 NL batting crown by a percentage point over Bottomley. Frisch was named the 1931 NL MVP.

In 1930, Philadelphia defeated St. Louis as Lefty Grove and George Earnshaw shut down the Cardinal offense in six games. The following season St. Louis won the World Championship in a seven-game series.

By 1933, Chick Hafey and Jim Bottomley had moved on to finish their careers elsewhere. Both men were later inducted into the Baseball Hall of Fame.

Frankie Frisch shows his method of stopping difficult grounders.

The Gashouse Gang

Frankie Frisch took over as Cardinals' player-manager midway through the 1933 season. The following year, the Redbirds roster gelled with an all-out style of play. The 1934 Cardinals were dubbed the "Gashouse Gang," for their mischievous antics both on and off the field.

With a cast of characters nicknamed Dizzy, Daffy, Ducky, Pepper, Lippy, and Ripper, the Gashouse Gang was one of the most memorable baseball teams ever. Winning 13 of their final 15 games in 1934, they overcame the New York Giants and took the NL Pennant.

Leading the Cards to over half of their victories that season were the Dean brothers from Lucas, Arkansas. Jay "Dizzy" Dean led the NL with 30 wins and 7 shutouts in 1934. He was also the league's top strikeout pitcher with 195 for the third straight time.

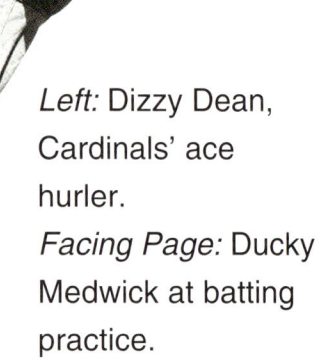

Left: Dizzy Dean, Cardinals' ace hurler.
Facing Page: Ducky Medwick at batting practice.

Dizzy was named the 1934 NL MVP. His younger brother, Paul "Daffy" Dean, recorded 19 victories and 150 strikeouts of his own, and was a key addition to the Cardinal staff.

First baseman James "Ripper" Collins ripped a league-leading 35 home runs in 1934. His .615 slugging average was also tops in the NL. Veteran John "Pepper" Martin played third base and led the NL in stolen bases for the second straight season. Martin was called "The Wild Horse of the Osage," as his head-first, reckless abandon on the basepaths defined the Gashouse Gang's style.

Another great player was shortstop Leo "Lippy" Durocher. Leo led the NL in fielding average three times.

The Cardinals met the AL Champion Detroit Tigers in the 1934 World Series. The series was tied at three games apiece when Dizzy

Left: Leo Durocher at bat. *Facing Page:* Dizzy Dean comes home on a double by Frankie Frisch during Game Seven of the 1934 World Series against the Detroit Tigers.

took the mound in Detroit for Game Seven. It was his third starting assignment in seven days.

Three days earlier Dean became truly dizzy when a relay throw hit him squarely in the forehead as he slid into second base. The St. Louis crowd was shocked as their star pitcher was carried off the field. He later eased everyone's tension, in his own humorous way, saying, "The doctors X-rayed my head and found nothing."

The Cardinals won the 1934 World Championship as Dizzy completed a six-hit shutout in the final game. The Dean brothers won two games each to secure the title for St. Louis.

Dizzy Dean led the NL again in 1935 with 28 wins and 190 strikeouts. A line drive off the bat of Hall-of-Famer Earl Averill in the 1937 All-Star Game broke Dizzy's toe, ending his days as the NL's most dominating pitcher.

Ducky Medwick was the NL's MVP in 1937. He won an NL Triple Crown with 31 HRs, 154 RBIs, and .374 batting average, as well as leading the league with a .988 fielding average.

The Gashouse Gang never won another pennant. Dizzy Dean, Ducky Medwick, Leo Durocher, and Frankie Frisch all became members of the Baseball Hall of Fame.

Pepper Martin scores a run in Game One of the 1934 World Series. Martin slid home after a single by Ducky Medwick.

St. Louis Cardinal outfielder Enos Slaughter.

Enos & The Man

The Cardinal farm system continued to produce top quality ballplayers into the 1940s. They won four more NL Pennants and three World Championships during that decade. Leading the way were a pair of Hall-of-Fame outfielders.

Enos "Country" Slaughter came up from the Cardinal "farm" in 1938. He quickly earned a reputation for his toughness and hustle. Slaughter was an All-Star outfielder 10 times. His career was interrupted by his three-year service in the U.S. military during World War II.

In 1941, Slaughter was joined in the Cardinal outfield by a baseball legend. Stan "The Man" Musial played 22 seasons with the

St. Louis

Second baseman Rogers Hornsby had a .424 batting average in 1924, the highest in modern baseball history.

Ducky Medwick was the NL's MVP in 1937.

Frankie Frisch was named the 1931 NL MVP.

Dizzy Dean and the rest of the "Gashouse Gang" won the 1934 World Series.

Cardinals

Hall-of-Famer Enos Slaughter came up from the Cardinal "farm" in 1938.

Lou Brock joined the Cardinals in 1964. He finished his career with 3,023 hits and 938 stolen bases.

In 1980, Ozzie Smith earned the first of 13 straight Gold Glove Awards.

Stan Musial was an NL All-Star 20 times. He joined the Cardinals in 1941.

Outfielder Lonnie Smith led the NL in runs with 120 in 1982.

Cardinals. He was an NL All-Star 20 times! He won the NL batting crown 7 times, led the NL in doubles 8 times, and finished with 1,951 RBIs. Musial's 3,630 career hits rank fourth on the all-time list, behind Pete Rose (4,256), Ty Cobb (4,189), and Hank Aaron (3,771).

The Cardinals won their first of three straight NL Pennants in 1942. Mort Cooper led the league with 22 wins and an ERA of 1.78 that year. Redbird rookie Johnny Beazley finished right behind Cooper in both categories. The Cards defeated Joe DiMaggio's New York Yankees in the 1942 World Series, four games to one.

In 1943, Enos Slaughter, along with hundreds of other major leaguers, went to war. Musial, who was drafted into the Navy two years later, won his first batting crown, and was the NL's MVP. The Cardinals took the NL Pennant by 18 games over the Cincinnati Reds. The Yankees avenged their World Series loss of 1942 by defeating the Redbirds in five games.

Sportsman's Park hosted all six games of the 1944 World Series, as the St. Louis Browns won their only AL Pennant. The Cardinals dropped two of the first three games, before winning three straight to gain their second World Championship in three years.

With Musial and Slaughter missing from the 1945 lineup, the Cards fell to second place in the NL. Both men returned in 1946, and

Stan Musial smacks a homer.

Enos Slaughter scores the winning run in the 1946 World Series game against the Boston Red Sox.

the Cardinals were back on top. Musial won his second NL MVP Award. Slaughter led the league with 130 RBIs, which was one of the few offensive categories Musial did not lead.

Albert "Red" Schoendienst was in his second season when the Cardinals defeated the Boston Red Sox in the 1946 World Series. He went on to lead NL second baseman in fielding average six times. The Redbirds never returned to the post-season in his 19-year playing career. Red Schoendienst managed the Cardinals for 14 seasons, beginning in 1965. He later joined Stan Musial and Enos Slaughter in the Baseball Hall of Fame.

New Owner

The St. Louis Cardinals were purchased by August Busch Jr. in 1953. Eleven years later "Augie" won his first baseball championship.

The Cards were in seventh place and playing below .500 in June, 1964. That month they sent pitcher Ernie Broglio to the Chicago Cubs for an unproven outfielder named Lou Brock.

Broglio had led the NL in wins in 1960. His trade was unpopular with Cardinal players and fans alike. Brock responded by batting .348 for the remainder of the season, and finishing second in the NL with 43 stolen bases.

The Cardinals rose to the top of the league, winning eight straight games in September. Third baseman Ken Boyer led the NL with 119 RBIs, while pitchers Ray Sadecki and Bob Gibson combined for

Lou Brock smacks one of his many hits for the St. Louis Cardinals.

39 victories. The Philadelphia Phillies lost 10 straight down the stretch, folding out of first place and handing the 1964 NL Pennant to St. Louis.

The Redbirds faced the New York Yankees in the World Series. Bob Gibson set the first of his many World Series records, with 31 strikeouts.

In Game Seven, Lou Brock and Ken Boyer homered for the Cards. Clete Boyer (Ken's brother) homered for the Yanks in the same game! Gibson held on for the victory, and St. Louis won their eighth World Championship.

The Cardinals brought up a 21-year-old left-hander named Steve Carlton in 1965. He pitched only 25 innings that year, striking out 21 batters. "Lefty" pitched seven seasons with the Cardinals, before joining the Philadelphia Phillies in 1972. He finished his Hall-of-Fame career with 4,136 strikeouts, second on the all-time list.

Busch Stadium opened in 1966. The next year, the Cards won the first of two straight NL Pennants. St. Louis finished 10.5 games in front of the San Francisco Giants in 1967, and defeated the Boston Red Sox in the World Series. Bob Gibson pitched 3 complete game victories in the series, allowing only 3 earned runs in 27 innings pitched.

Gibson was the NL Cy Young Award winner in 1968. He led the league with 13 shutouts and 268 strikeouts. His 1.12 ERA that season was the lowest in 54 years, and has never been matched! In the World Series, Gibson continued to rewrite the record books.

The Detroit Tigers won the 1968 AL Pennant, as Denny McLain's 31 wins were the most in 37 years. In the "Year of the Pitcher," it was McLain versus Gibson in the World Series!

Gibson won the first game with a five-hit shutout, and set a World Series record for strikeouts with 17. In Game Four, he set two more records, with his seventh consecutive World Series victory, and his second World Series home run (a record for pitchers).

The Tigers defeated Gibson and the Cardinals in Game Seven to become World Champions. Bob Gibson struck out 35 batters in the series, breaking a record he set four years earlier.

While Gibson was setting records on the mound, Lou Brock was breaking them on the basepaths. Brock finished his career with 3,023 hits and led the NL in stolen bases 8 times. He stole more bases in 1974 than any other NL player this century! Brock's 938 career stolen bases currently ranks second on the all-time list, behind Rickey Henderson.

Lou Brock and Bob Gibson were both elected to the Hall of Fame in their first year of eligibility.

Bob Gibson, Hall-of-Fame pitcher for the St. Louis Cardinals.

Come To See The Wizard

The Cardinals became members of the NL East when divisional play began in 1969. They finished second three times in the 1970s, before taking their first NL East Division Championship in 1982.

St. Louis returned to their long tradition of winning games with defense and speed in the 1980s. Veteran outfielder Lonnie Smith finished second in the league with 68 stolen bases, and led the NL in runs with 120 in 1982. As a team, the Cardinals led the league in fielding average and stolen bases.

Keith Hernandez won the fifth of his 11 straight Gold Glove Awards at first base. A rookie center fielder and an acrobatic shortstop joined Hernandez in 1982.

Willie McGee won two NL batting crowns, two Gold Glove Awards, and an NL MVP Award while playing center field for the Cardinals. His tremendous speed was utilized on the basepaths, as well as for turning long fly-balls into outs.

Willie McGee goes to the wall attempting to haul in a long fly ball by Gary Gaetti of the Minnesota Twins.

Osborne "Ozzie" Smith came to the Cards in a trade with the San Diego Padres. "The Wizard" soon became a fan favorite, as he back-flipped into position before every home game, and converted seemingly impossible defensive plays. In 1982, Ozzie earned the third of his 13 straight Gold Glove Awards, and the Cardinals returned to the post-season.

The 1982 National League Championship Series (NLCS) matched the Cardinals with the Atlanta Braves. St. Louis reliever Bruce Sutter, who led the NL in saves with 36 for the fourth consecutive year, pitched 4.1 hitless innings in the playoffs. The Redbirds swept the Braves and landed back in the World Series.

The Milwaukee Brewers were the 1982 AL Champions. They destroyed the Cards 10-0 in Game One. St. Louis came from behind to take Game Two, and hung on to win their tenth World Championship in seven games.

The Cardinals added another speedster to their lineup three years later. Vince Coleman was the NL Rookie of the Year in 1985. He was the first NL player to steal 100 or more bases in a season since Lou Brock. Coleman led the NL in stolen bases for six straight years.

St. Louis returned to the World Series two more times in the 1980s. In 1985, they lost to their Missouri counterparts, the Kansas City Royals, in a seven-game "Show-Me Showdown." Two years later they were defeated in another seven game struggle by the Minnesota Twins.

Facing page: Ozzie Smith watches the ball after hitting a sacrifice fly in a game against the Chicago Cubs.
Right: Lonnie Smith beats the tag of Phillies' Ivan DeJesus after stealing second.

Outfielder Brian Jordan stands in the Cardinals' dugout in a game against the New York Mets.

Tradition Of Excellence

The St. Louis Cardinals have won nine World Championships, more than any other NL team. Their first World Series title (and tenth overall) came as members of the old AA, more than 100 years ago!

The Redbirds moved into the new NL Central Division in 1994. Today they are mixing some old tradition with young talent in hopes of recapturing past glories.

Royce Clayton will compete for the starting shortstop role with Ozzie Smith. Willie McGee will return to the Cards in 1996, after five seasons of playing elsewhere. Tony LaRussa takes over as Cardinals manager, after several successful seasons managing the Oakland Athletics.

LaRussa will look for young stars, like Brian Jordan, Bernard Gilkey, and Ray Lankford to bring St. Louis another baseball championship. Fans of the Cardinals hold high expectations. Their team has a tradition of excellence!

All-Star: A player who is voted by fans as the best player at one position in a given year.

American League (AL): An association of baseball teams formed in 1900 which make up one-half of the major leagues.

American League Championship Series (ALCS): A best- of- seven game playoff with the winner going to the World Series to face the National League Champions.

Batting Average: A baseball statistic calculated by dividing a batter's hits by the number of times at bat.

Earned Run Average (ERA): A baseball statistic which calculates the average number of runs a pitcher gives up per nine innings of work.

Fielding Average: A baseball statistic which calculates a fielder's success rate based on the number of chances the fielder has to record an out.

Hall of Fame: A memorial for the greatest baseball players of all time located in Cooperstown, New York.

Home Run (HR): A play in baseball where a batter hits the ball over the outfield fence scoring everyone on base as well as the batter.

Major Leagues: The highest ranking associations of professional baseball teams in the world, currently consisting of the American and National Baseball Leagues.

Minor Leagues: A system of professional baseball leagues at levels below Major League Baseball.

National League (NL): An association of baseball teams formed in 1876 which make up one-half of the major leagues.

National League Championship Series (NLCS): A best- of- seven game playoff with the winner going to the World Series to face the American League Champions.

Pennant: A flag which symbolizes the championship of a professional baseball league.

Pitcher: The player on a baseball team who throws the ball for the batter to hit. The pitcher stands on a mound and pitches the ball toward the strike zone area above the plate.

Plate: The place on a baseball field where a player stands to bat. It is used to determine the width of the strike zone. Forming the point of the diamond-shaped field, it is the final goal a base runner must reach to score a run.

RBI: A baseball statistic standing for *runs batted in.* Players receive an RBI for each run that scores on their hits.

Rookie: A first-year player, especially in a professional sport.

Slugging Percentage: A statistic which points out a player's ability to hit for extra bases by taking the number of total bases hit and dividing it by the number of at-bats.

Stolen Base: A play in baseball when a base runner advances to the next base while the pitcher is delivering a pitch.

Strikeout: A play in baseball when a batter is called out for failing to put the ball in play after the pitcher has delivered three strikes.

Triple Crown: A rare accomplishment when a single player finishes a season leading the league in batting average, home runs, and RBIs. A pitcher can win a Triple Crown by leading the league in wins, ERA, and strikeouts.

Walk: A play in baseball when a batter receives four pitches out of the strike zone and is allowed to go to first base.

World Series: The championship of Major League Baseball played since 1903 between the pennant winners from the American and National Leagues.

Index

A
Aaron, Hank   20
Alexander, Grover Cleveland "Pete"   9
All Star   16, 17, 20
American Association (AA)   4, 6, 28
American League (AL)   11, 16, 20, 23, 27
Atlanta Braves   27
Averill, Earl   16

B
Beazley, Johnny   20
Boston Red Sox   21, 23
Bottomley, Jim   9, 10, 11
Boyer, Clete   23
Boyer, Ken   22, 23
Brock, Lou   4, 22, 23, 24, 27
Broglio, Ernie   22
Brown Stockings   4, 6, 7
Busch, August Jr.   22
Busch Stadium   23

C
Carlton, Steve   23
Chicago Cubs   22
Chicago White Stockings   6
Cincinnati Reds   9, 20
Clayton, Royce   28
Cleveland Spiders   7
Cobb, Ty   20
Coleman, Vince   27
Collins, James "Ripper"   14
Cooper, Mort   20

D
Dean, Jay "Dizzy"   12, 14, 16
Dean, Paul "Daffy"   12, 14
Detroit Tigers   16, 23
Detroit Wolverines   6
Durocher, Leo "Lippy"   14, 16

E
Earnshaw, George   11

F
Frisch, Frankie   10, 11, 12, 16

G
Gashouse Gang   4, 12, 16
Gibson, Bob   4, 22, 23, 24
Gilkey, Bernard   4, 28
Grove, Lefty   11

31

H
Hafey, Charles "Chick" 9, 10, 11
Hall of Fame 9, 11, 16, 17, 21, 23, 24
Hallahan, "Wild Bill" 11
Henderson, Rickey 24
Hernandez, Keith 25
Hornsby, Rogers 4, 9, 10

J
Jordan, Brian 4, 28

L
Lankford, Ray 4, 28
LaRussa, Tony 28

M
Martin, John "Pepper" 14
McGee, Willie 25, 28
McLain, Denny 23
Medwick, Joe "Ducky" 16
Milwaukee Brewers 27
Minnesota Twins 27
Musial, Stan 4, 17, 20, 21

N
National League (NL) 4, 6, 7, 9, 10, 11, 12, 14, 16, 17, 20, 21, 22, 23, 24, 25, 27, 28
National League Championship Series (NLCS) 27
New York Giants 6, 10, 12
New York Yankees 9, 11, 20, 23

P
Philadelphia Phillies 22, 23

R
Rickey, Branch 7
Rose, Pete 20

S
Sadecki, Ray 22
San Diego Padres 27
San Francisco Giants 23
Schoendienst, Albert "Red" 21
Slaughter, Enos "Country" 17, 20, 21
Smith, Lonnie 25
Smith, Ozzie 4, 27, 28
Sportsman's Park 9, 20
St. Louis Perfectos 4
Sutter, Bruce 27

W
World Series 4, 6, 9, 11, 16, 20, 21, 23, 27, 28
World War II 17